# Go Flight

Level 5H

Written by Lucy George
Illustrated by Monica Armino
Reading Consultant: Betty Franchi

CALGARY PUBLIC LIBRARY

FEB 2014

# About Phonics

Spoken English uses more than 40 speech sounds. Each sound is called a *phoneme*. Some phonemes relate to a single letter (d-o-g) and others to combinations of letters (sh-ar-p). When a phoneme is written down, it is called a *grapheme*. Teaching these sounds, matching them to their written form, and sounding out words for reading is the basis of phonics.

Early phonics instruction gives children the tools to sound out, blend, and say the words without having to rely on memory or guesswork. This instruction gives children the confidence and ability to read unfamiliar words, helping them progress toward independent reading.

# About the Consultant

Betty Franchi is an American educator with a Bachelor's Degree in Elementary and Middle Education as well as a Master's Degree in Special Education. Betty holds a National Boards for Professional Teaching Standards certification. Throughout her 24 years as a teacher, she has studied and developed an expertise in Phonetic Awareness and has implemented phonetic strategies, teaching many young children to read, including students with special needs.

# Reading tips

This book focuses on the *s* sound
(made with the letters *se*) as in hou**se**.

## Tricky and/or new words in this book

Any words in bold may have unusual spellings
or are new and have not yet been introduced.

> **Tricky and/or new words in this book**
>
> **come  vegetation  warmer
> groups  worse  their
> course  bodies**

## Extra ways to have fun with this book

After the readers have read the story, ask them
questions about what they have just read.

*Why do geese fly south for the winter?*
*What new words did you learn in this book?*

We fly a long way
south, but it's worth it
for the weather.

# A Pronunciation Guide

This grid contains the sounds used in the stories in levels 4, 5, and 6 and a guide on how to say them.

| | | | |
|---|---|---|---|
| /ă/ as in pat | /ā/ as in pay | /âr/ as in care | /ä/ as in father |
| /b/ as in bib | /ch/ as in church | /d/ as in deed/ milled | /ĕ/ as in pet |
| /ē/ as in bee | /f/ as in fife/ phase/ rough | /g/ as in gag | /h/ as in hat |
| /hw/ as in which | /ĭ/ as in pit | /ī/ as in pie/ by | /îr/ as in pier |
| /j/ as in judge | /k/ as in kick/ cat/ pique | /l/ as in lid/ needle (nēd'l) | /m/ as in mom |
| /n/ as in no/ sudden (sŭd'n) | /ng/ as in thing | /ŏ/ as in pot | /ō/ as in toe |
| /ô/ as in caught/ paw/ for/ horrid/ hoarse | /oi/ as in noise | /ʊ/ as in took | /ū/ as in cute |

| /ou/ as in **ou**t | /p/ as in **p**o**p** | /r/ as in **r**oa**r** | /s/ as in **s**au**c**e |
|---|---|---|---|
| /sh/ as in **sh**ip/ di**sh** | /t/ as in **t**igh**t**/ stopp**ed** | /th/ as in **th**in | /th/ as in **th**is |
| /ŭ/ as in c**u**t | /ûr/ as in **ur**ge/ t**er**m/ f**ir**m/ w**or**d/ h**ear**d | /v/ as in **v**al**ve** | /w/ as in **w**ith |
| /y/ as in **y**es | /z/ as in **z**ebra/ **x**ylem | /zh/ as in vi**s**ion/ plea**s**ure/ gara**ge**/ | /ə/ as in **a**bout/ it**e**m/ **e**dible/ gall**o**p/ circ**u**s |
| /ər/ as in butt**er** | | | |

Be careful not to add an /uh/ sound to /s/, /t/, /p/, /c/, /h/, /r/, /m/, /d/, /g/, /l/, /f/ and /b/. For example, say /fff/ not /fuh/ and /sss/ not /suh/.

The geese gather, getting ready
for a great journey.

Now that winter has **come** to the north, the **vegetation** is sparse and snow lies on the ground.

The geese gather at the top
of a cliff to fly south for
the winter.

They will fly south until they find a place with more food and **warmer** weather.

The cold winds chase them away as they fly in dense **groups**, leaving before the weather gets **worse**.

They travel over snow
and water, but little else.

**Their** wings pulse and beat against the wind.

As they fly south, the air grows warmer, and the terrain grows more diverse.

Soon, they see coarse
grass and flowers.

They still fly with purpose,
keeping their **course**.

The geese sense their way south,
seeking the warm plains.

Finally, after their immense journey over a vast expanse of the globe, they arrive in a pond.

They rinse their tired **bodies** and immerse themselves in the water.

Here, food is not sparse.
It is plentiful, and the
geese honk happily.

They will stay here, where it's warm, until summer comes to the north again.

They will fly the whole
journey again, in reverse,
when summer comes to
the north again.

# OVER 48 TITLES IN SIX LEVELS
## Betty Franchi recommends...

### Some titles from Level 4

The Circus Mice — 978 1 84898 783 8

Monster's Night — 978 1 84898 784 5

Jemima The Spy — 978 1 84898 785 2

### Other titles to enjoy from Level 5

The Gigantic Bear — 978 1 84898 787 6

Celebrity Celia — 978 1 84898 788 3

The Cemetery Dance — 978 1 84898 789 0

### Some titles from Level 6

Hugh is New — 978 1 84898 791 3

Clumsy Eagle — 978 1 84898 792 0

Bad Zombie Movie — 978 1 84898 793 7

An Hachette Company
First published in the United States by TickTock, an imprint of Octopus Publishing Group.
www.octopusbooksusa.com

Copyright © Octopus Publishing Group Ltd 2013

Distributed in the US by
Hachette Book Group USA
237 Park Avenue, New York NY 10017, USA

Distributed in Canada by
Canadian Manda Group
165 Dufferin Street, Toronto, Ontario, Canada M6K 3H6

ISBN 978 1 84898 790 6

Printed and bound in China
10 9 8 7 6 5 4 3 2 1

All rights reserved. No part of this work may be reproduced or utilized in any form or by any means,
electronic or mechanical, including photocopying, recording, or by any information storage and retrieval system,
without the prior written permission of the publisher.